The Miracle of Helen the Rabbit

by Steve Rogers

Strategic Book Publishing and Rights Co.

Strategic Book Publishing and Rights Co., LLC
USA | Singapore
www.sbpra.com

For information about special discounts for bulk purchases, please contact Strategic Book Publishing and Rights Co. Special Sales, at bookorder@sbpra.net.

ISBN: 978-1-949483-42-0

Book Design: Suzanne Kelly

A special thank you to my talented cover artist Maura Collins. Her imagination and creativity really shined through in her cover creation.

Maura is an eighth grade high honors student at Thompson Middle School in Middletown, New Jersey. She was selected by her school faculty as a tutor for her classmates because of her A+ grade average.

Maura is both an animal lover and advocate. She is both an artist and a guitar player. She has created brilliant documentaries. She enjoys golf, running and yoga.

If it hasn't happened by the time she is eligible, she'll be the first woman to be President.

May 10, 1957

Dear Mother,
I love you very much.
I will try to be good.
And I will work hard in School.
        love
        Stephen

Dedication

This book is dedicated to my mother, Helen Rogers, currently residing somewhere in heaven along with my dad, Tom. She was and is a very special woman who gave her all for her family. She put up with a lot when my brothers and sisters, Tom, Dan, Pat, and Kathy were growing up, especially from me. Mom, we love you and miss you, and are thrilled you decided to come back to us as a bunny rabbit.

Preface

The scene of the Miracle! Helen the Rabbit appeared out of nowhere on the left side of this ratty old chair adorned with duct tape. How did she get there?

Sometimes things happen in our lives we can't understand or believe. Sort of like UFOs—those things people see in the sky they think come from other planets. Maybe they do. I wouldn't know. I do know there are such things as we call miracles. Once upon a time I never believed in them. I do now. Take my word for it.

Reincarnation: Ever hear the word? It is when a person dies and comes back as someone or something else. Maybe you were a hippopotamus in a past life. Maybe a kangaroo came back as your little sister. If the person is someone you love, they will always come back to you as someone or something else.

Pay attention, because the miracle I told you about could happen to you just like it did to me.

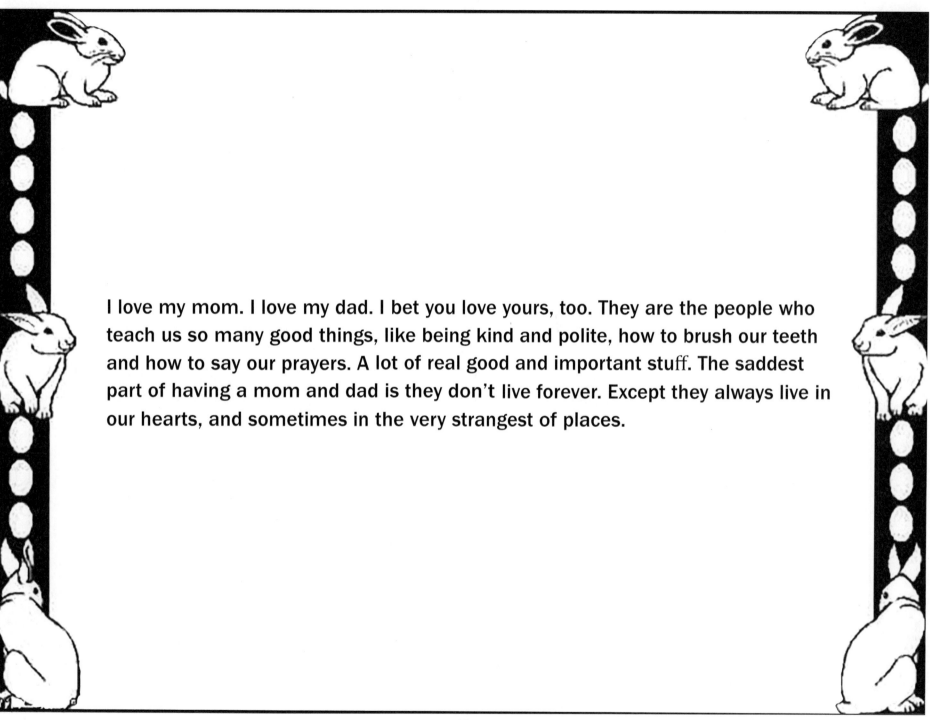

I love my mom. I love my dad. I bet you love yours, too. They are the people who teach us so many good things, like being kind and polite, how to brush our teeth and how to say our prayers. A lot of real good and important stuff. The saddest part of having a mom and dad is they don't live forever. Except they always live in our hearts, and sometimes in the very strangest of places.

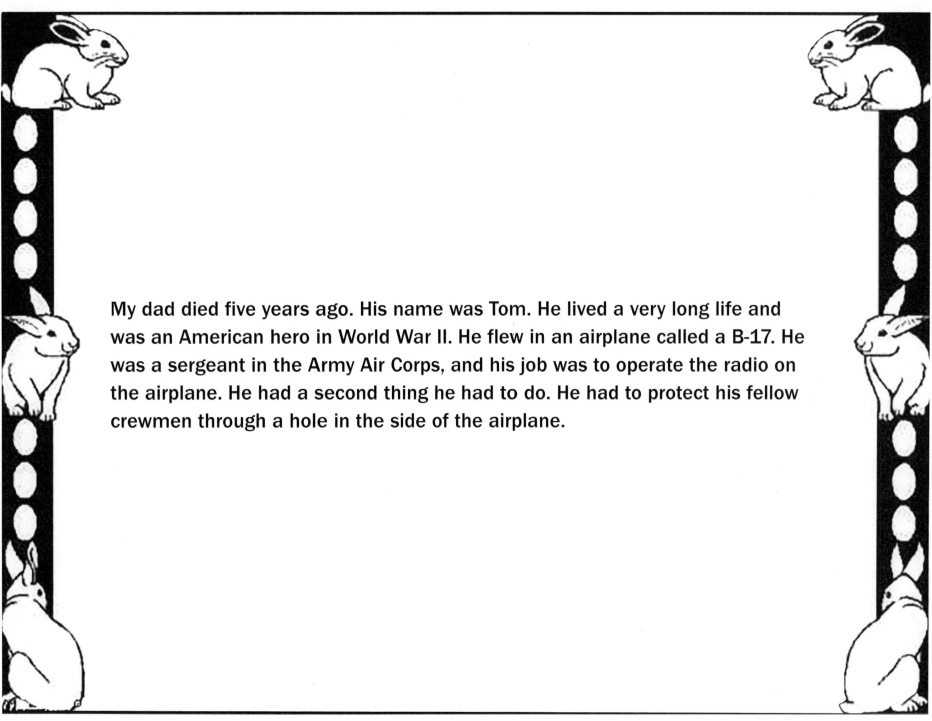

My dad died five years ago. His name was Tom. He lived a very long life and was an American hero in World War II. He flew in an airplane called a B-17. He was a sergeant in the Army Air Corps, and his job was to operate the radio on the airplane. He had a second thing he had to do. He had to protect his fellow crewmen through a hole in the side of the airplane.

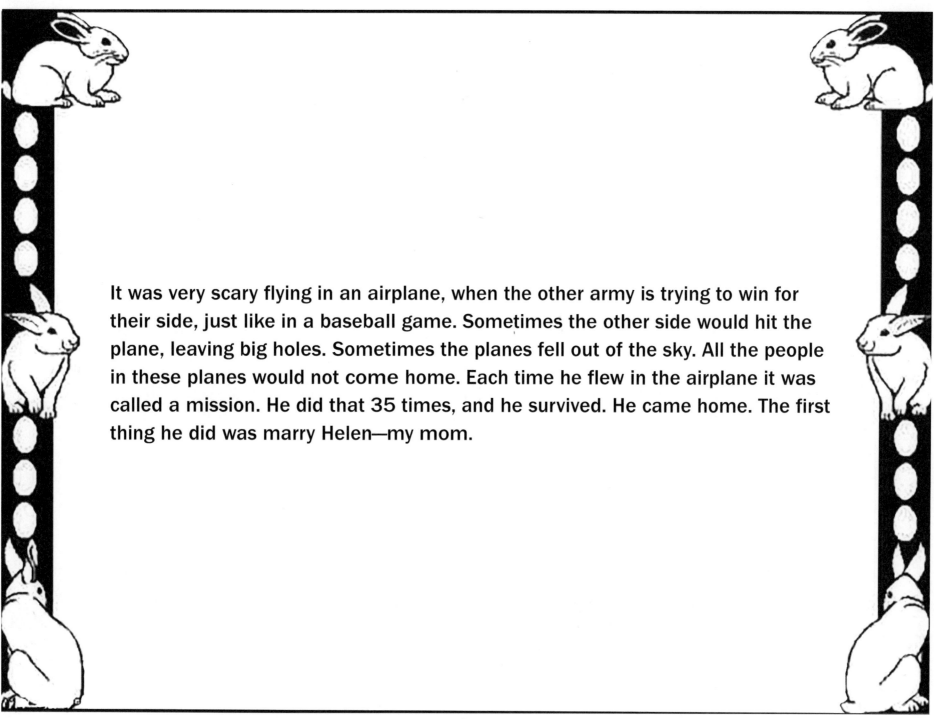

It was very scary flying in an airplane, when the other army is trying to win for their side, just like in a baseball game. Sometimes the other side would hit the plane, leaving big holes. Sometimes the planes fell out of the sky. All the people in these planes would not come home. Each time he flew in the airplane it was called a mission. He did that 35 times, and he survived. He came home. The first thing he did was marry Helen—my mom.

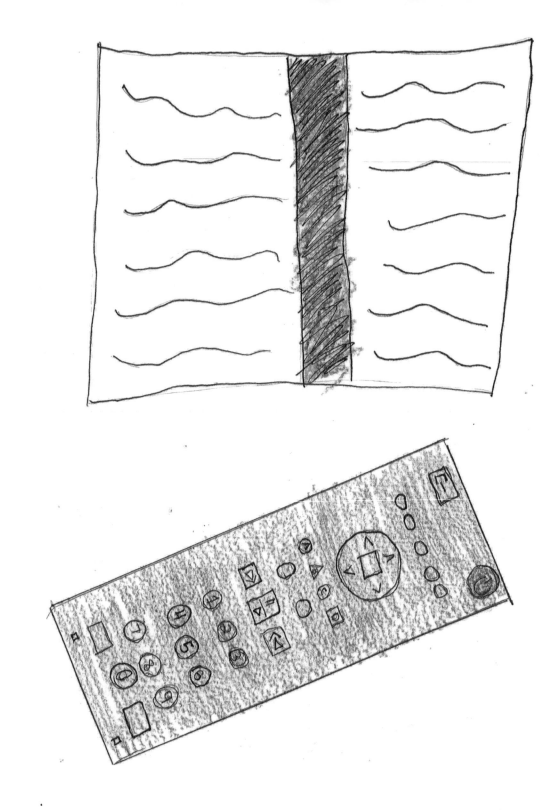

Soon the family grew. Tom came first. Then me, Patty, Dan, and finally Kathy. It was a good life for the family. There wasn't a lot of money to buy stuff, but we were blessed with something far more valuable: Imagination!! What a wonderful gift. We played outside every day and used that gift to make up games to play and adventures to experience. No computers, PlayStations, cell phones, play dates and one hour of TV a day. How's that sound? It was the most fun you could ever have!! I know, because I was right in the middle of all that fun.

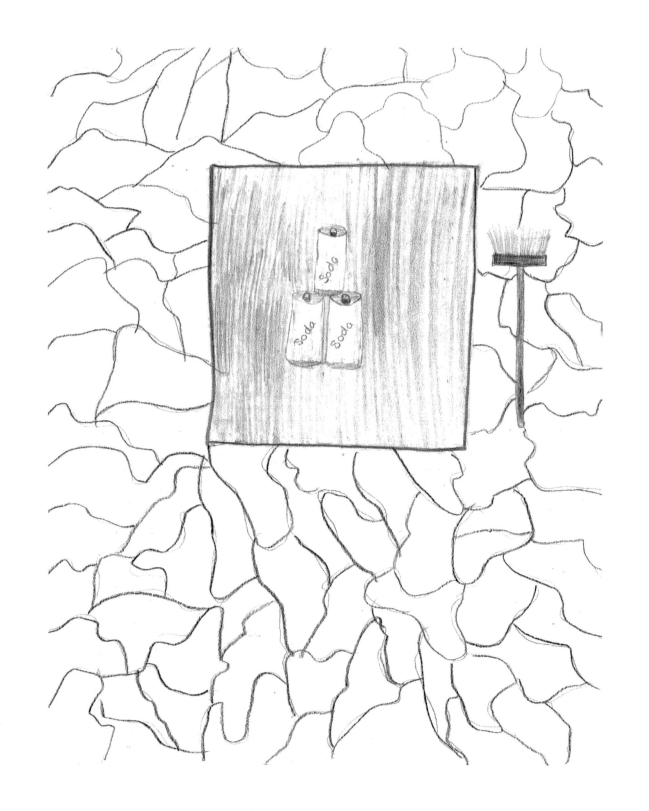

Remember I said imagination. We made up a game we called "cans." It was a combination of baseball, bowling, and cricket. Cricket is a game played in England. Cans was much more fun. It didn't require much in the way of equipment: two old broomsticks that were our bats, six empty soda cans, and a rubber ball. We would draw two squares with chalk in the middle of the street. The squares were about 30 feet apart. Right behind the squares we would set up three cans—two on the bottom and the third on top of them. There were two two-person teams. The team that was up to the plate or batting held the broomsticks. The other team lined up behind the cans and "pitched" a rubber ball like a bowling ball, trying to knock over the cans. The team at bat would try to hit the ball like swinging a golf club. If they missed and the ball hit the cans, that would be an out. If the batter hit the ball, then he would run to the other square and touch it with his stick, and his teammate would run from the opposite base and do the same thing. Each time they touched the base, they scored a run. The other team would run after the ball that was hit. They had to pick it up and run back to the base and knock over the cans to stop the other team from scoring more runs. When the pitching team got three outs on the batting team, they would switch places. It was the best game ever. If you try it someday, be sure you set up your field in a safe place where there are no cars that could interrupt your fun.

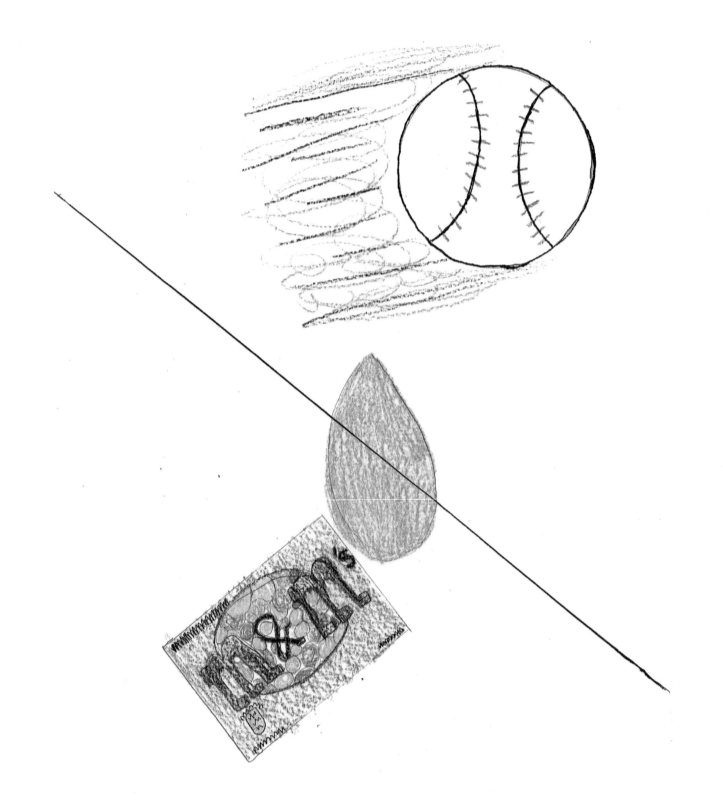

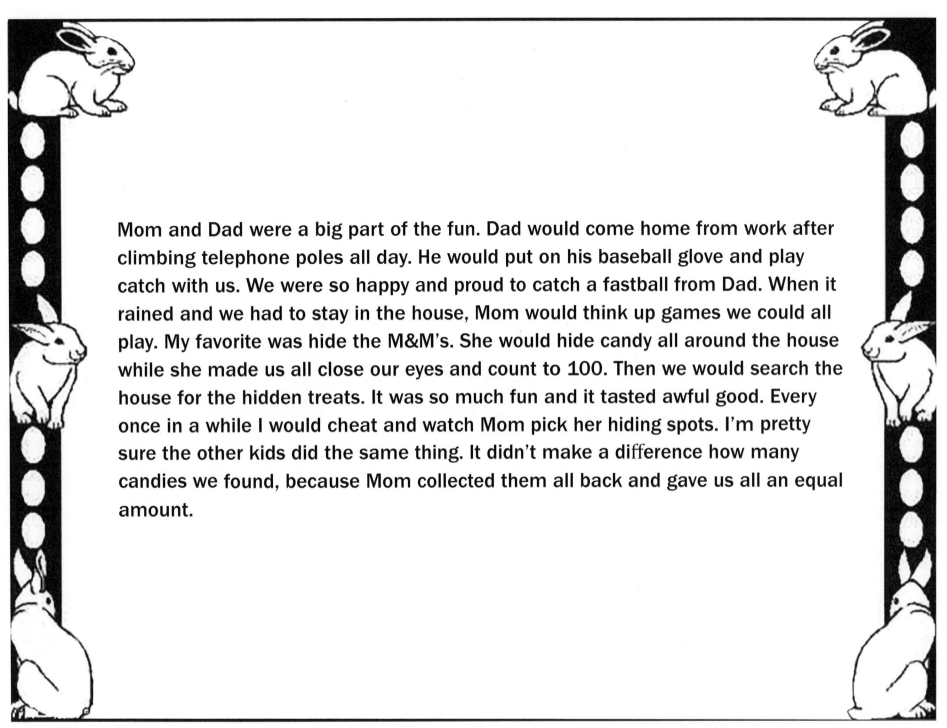

Mom and Dad were a big part of the fun. Dad would come home from work after climbing telephone poles all day. He would put on his baseball glove and play catch with us. We were so happy and proud to catch a fastball from Dad. When it rained and we had to stay in the house, Mom would think up games we could all play. My favorite was hide the M&M's. She would hide candy all around the house while she made us all close our eyes and count to 100. Then we would search the house for the hidden treats. It was so much fun and it tasted awful good. Every once in a while I would cheat and watch Mom pick her hiding spots. I'm pretty sure the other kids did the same thing. It didn't make a difference how many candies we found, because Mom collected them all back and gave us all an equal amount.

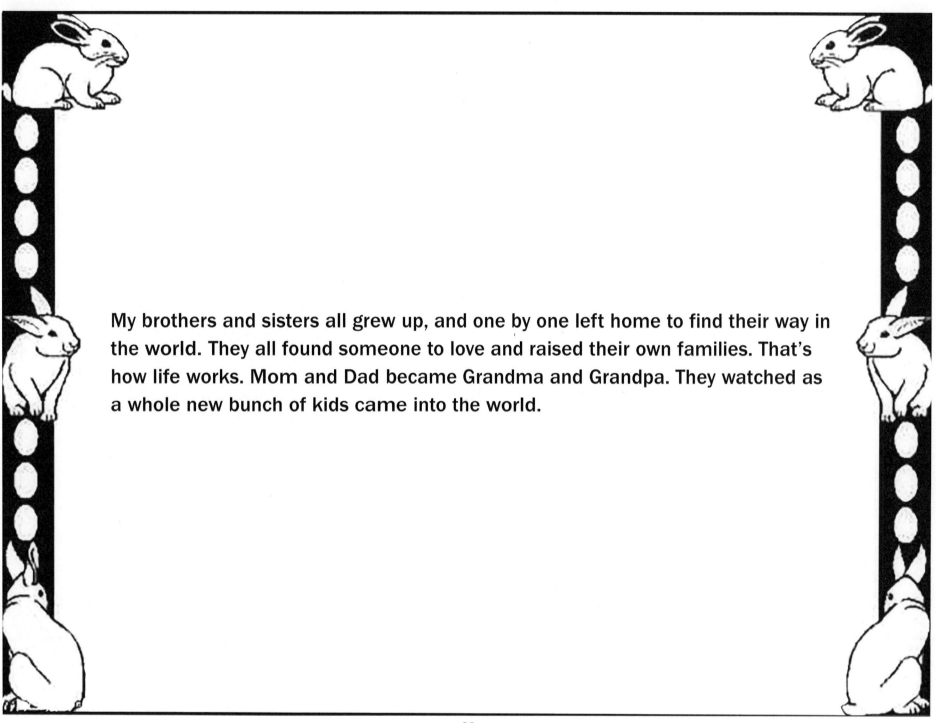

My brothers and sisters all grew up, and one by one left home to find their way in the world. They all found someone to love and raised their own families. That's how life works. Mom and Dad became Grandma and Grandpa. They watched as a whole new bunch of kids came into the world.

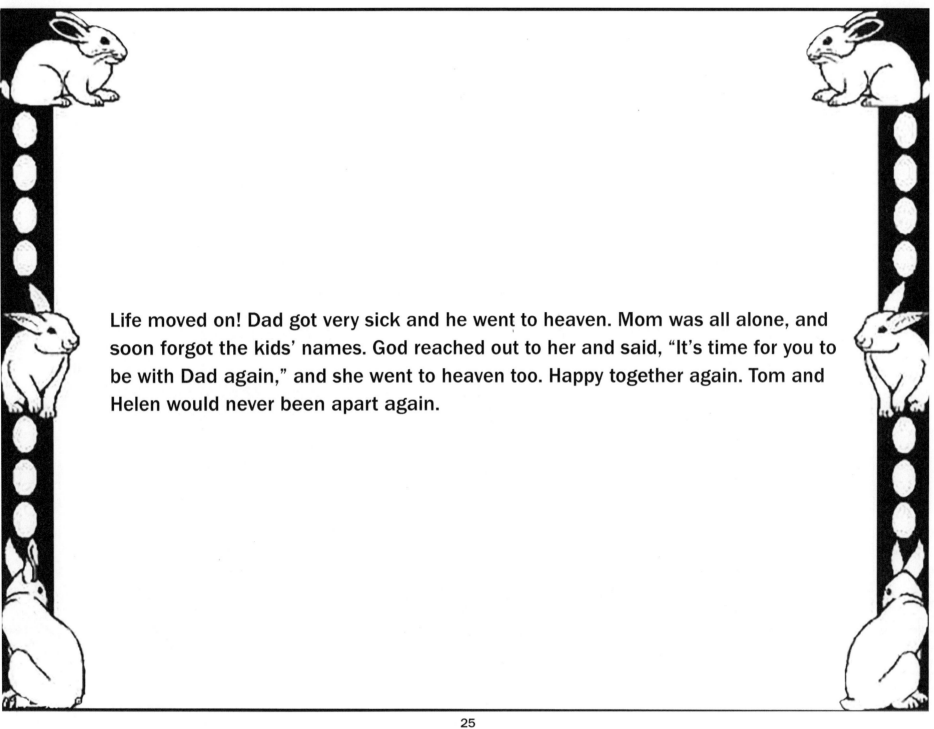

Life moved on! Dad got very sick and he went to heaven. Mom was all alone, and soon forgot the kids' names. God reached out to her and said, "It's time for you to be with Dad again," and she went to heaven too. Happy together again. Tom and Helen would never been apart again.

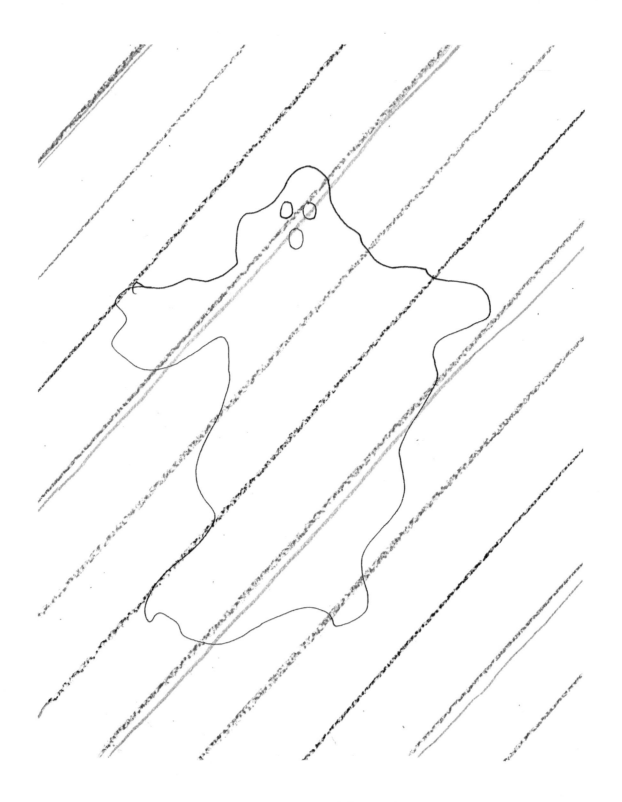

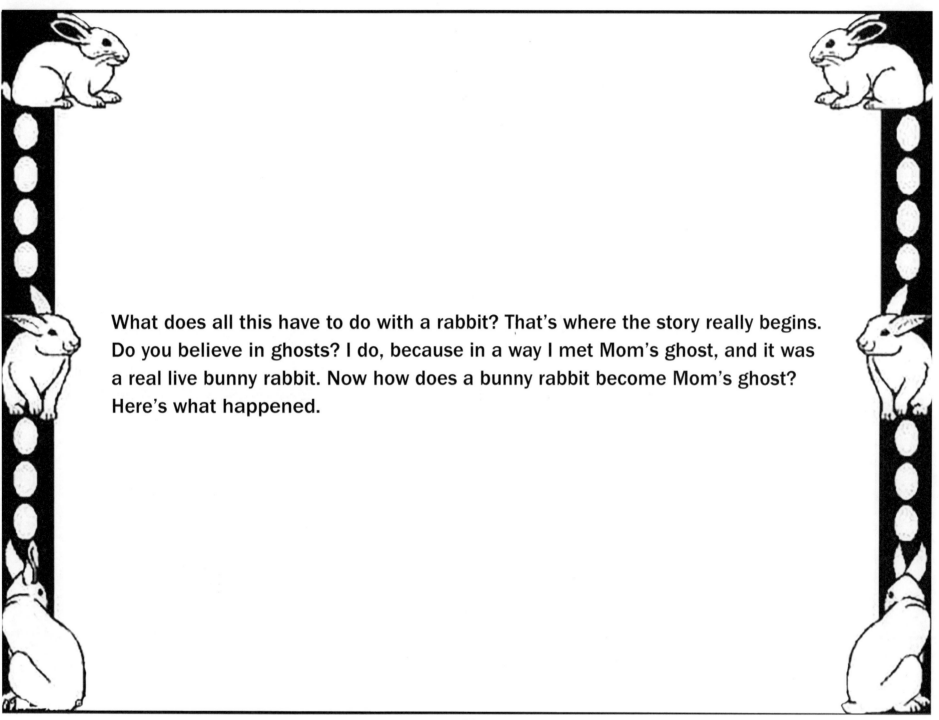

What does all this have to do with a rabbit? That's where the story really begins. Do you believe in ghosts? I do, because in a way I met Mom's ghost, and it was a real live bunny rabbit. Now how does a bunny rabbit become Mom's ghost? Here's what happened.

Two days after Mom went to heaven, I was sitting in my garage in my recliner. Have you ever heard of a man cave? It was my special alone place. A lot of dads have them. That makes a lot of moms very happy. Well, the garage was my man cave. I had a television, a telephone, a rocking chair Mom used to rock in, and a heater for when it got cold. I had a refrigerator, a radio, and a gadget called Alexa who I talked to every day. The best part was I had a dog that hung out with me every day. Doolin was a twelve-year-old Goldendoodle. He was my best buddy, who picked me as his guy the first time I met him at the kennel. He also was my traveling companion at my job. We would get in a car every work day and visit offices, where my business clients were far happier to see the dog than me. Dogs are easier to like than people on most work days.

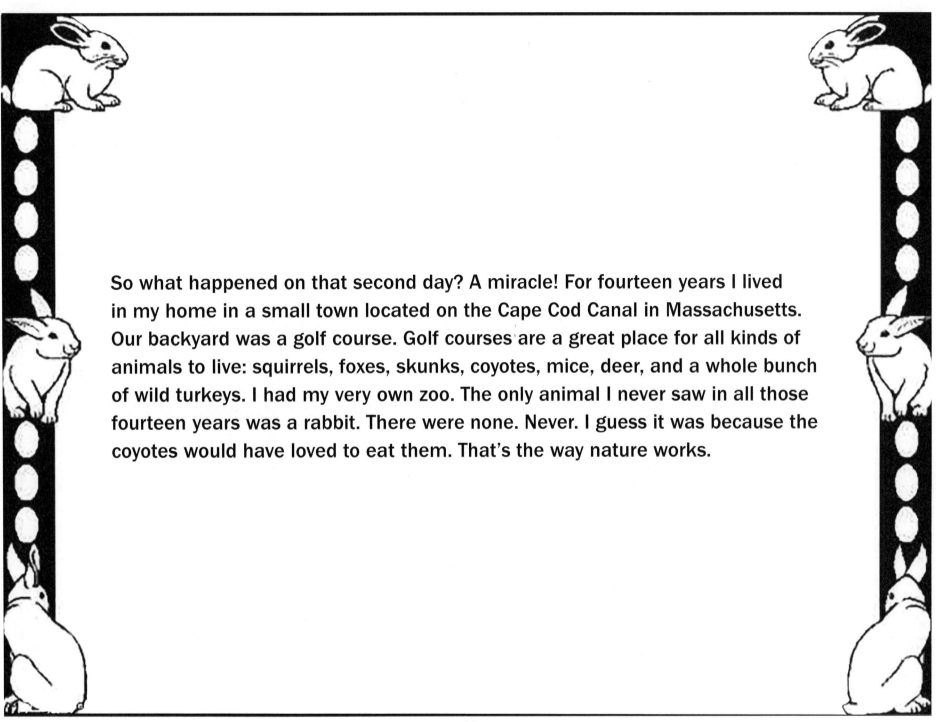

So what happened on that second day? A miracle! For fourteen years I lived in my home in a small town located on the Cape Cod Canal in Massachusetts. Our backyard was a golf course. Golf courses are a great place for all kinds of animals to live: squirrels, foxes, skunks, coyotes, mice, deer, and a whole bunch of wild turkeys. I had my very own zoo. The only animal I never saw in all those fourteen years was a rabbit. There were none. Never. I guess it was because the coyotes would have loved to eat them. That's the way nature works.

Back to the recliner.

I was reading a newspaper and listening to the radio. I saw something out of the corner of my eye while I was having sad thoughts about Mom. On the floor of the man cave was a full-grown rabbit. It was just sitting there quietly. I was shocked! What was a rabbit doing in my garage just sitting right next to me? And why wasn't it running away?

I bent down and picked up the rabbit and put it in my lap. It just sat and let me pet it. Doolin came over to the chair and licked it. The rabbit didn't move. How did it get there, and why was it acting like that? That's where the ghost part comes in. The garage door was always closed. The window was always shut. How did it get into the garage? It got there because it was a ghost—the ghost of my Mom, Helen. What else could it have been? That is the only explanation I can give you.

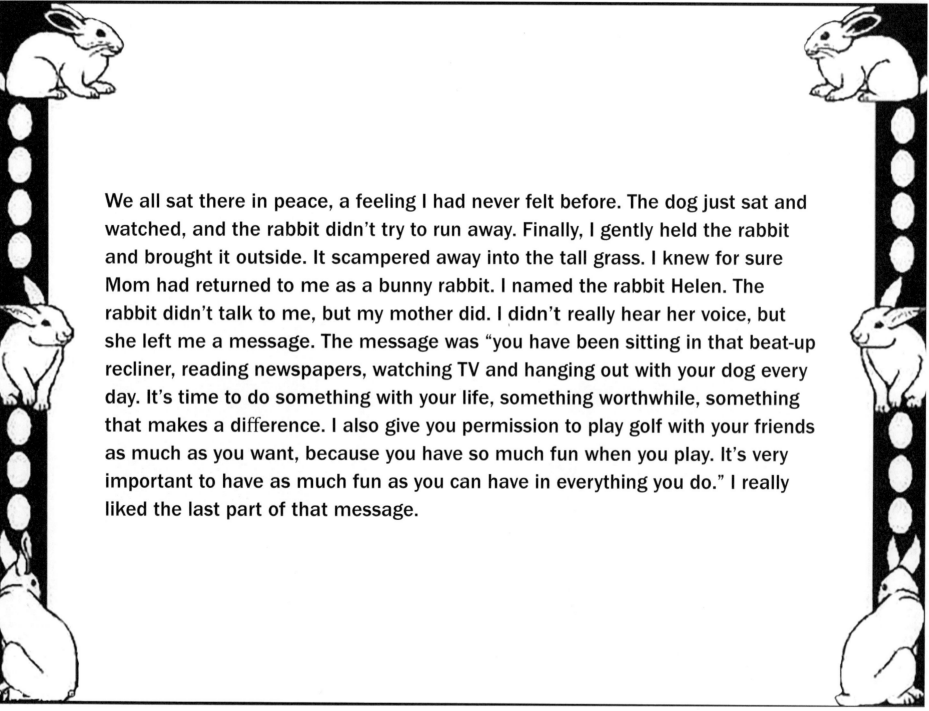

We all sat there in peace, a feeling I had never felt before. The dog just sat and watched, and the rabbit didn't try to run away. Finally, I gently held the rabbit and brought it outside. It scampered away into the tall grass. I knew for sure Mom had returned to me as a bunny rabbit. I named the rabbit Helen. The rabbit didn't talk to me, but my mother did. I didn't really hear her voice, but she left me a message. The message was "you have been sitting in that beat-up recliner, reading newspapers, watching TV and hanging out with your dog every day. It's time to do something with your life, something worthwhile, something that makes a difference. I also give you permission to play golf with your friends as much as you want, because you have so much fun when you play. It's very important to have as much fun as you can have in everything you do." I really liked the last part of that message.

So the next day I did what she told me to do. Always obey your mother! Now I like golf a whole lot, but to be honest I wasn't very good at it. When you get old and become a grandfather, you can't do the stuff you did when you were a kid, like playing basketball and baseball and football and soccer. But you can play golf, so that's what I did. The very next day I went to my golf course to play with my friends. One of my very best friends was a guy named "Two-Down Louie." He got that name because he always won and always collected the prize money. The name of our golf course was "Outlaw National." That wasn't the real name, but the name we gave it because it was filled with outlaws and outlaws in training.

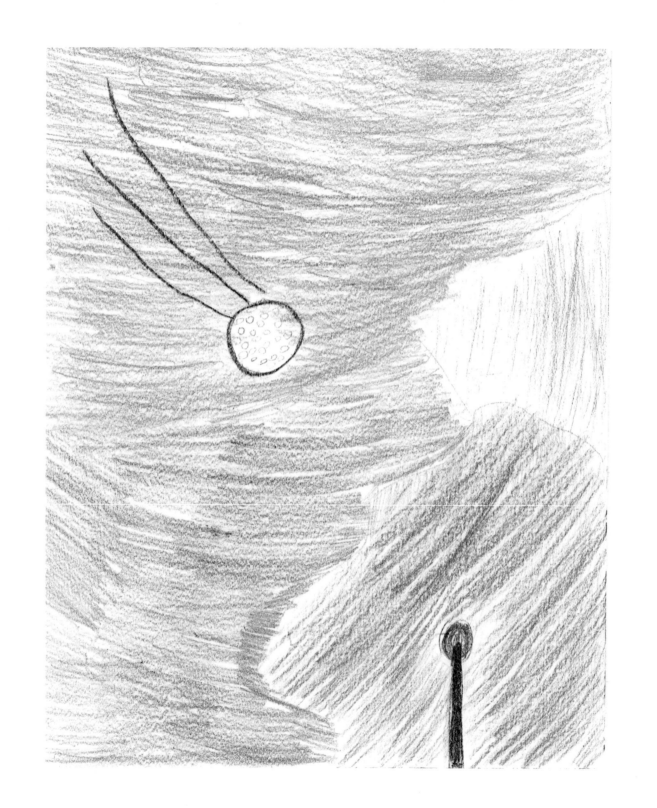

One of the holes was a par 3. Par 3 means you are supposed to be able to put the ball in the golf hole in 3 shots. It was 175 yards long and uphill. Remember, I told you I wasn't a very good golfer. My usual score was 5, which is called a double bogey. Anyway, Two-Down hit first, and as usual it was a good shot that looked like it hit the green. It was hard to tell; we couldn't really see the green because it was high up the hill. It was my turn. I took out my trusty 5 iron I usually did poorly with, but on that day I remembered what my mother told me. Have fun. I swung the club, and to my surprise I hit a shot directly at the flagstick. A flagstick is a pole with a flag on it that marks where the hole is. Wow! "I think I put it on the green for the first time in my life!" We high-fived to celebrate.

We got in the golf cart and drove up the hill. When we got to the green, only one ball was on the green, and it belonged to Louie. I must have hit it over the green and rolled it into the tall grass behind the green. I got out of the cart. I was very disappointed my ball was not on the green. I walked over to the tall grass and couldn't find the ball. Not only did I not land on the green, I lost my ball. The reason I couldn't find it was it was in the hole where the flagstick was. A hole in one!!!!! My very first one! Louie gave me a big hug, and I looked up at the sky and said, "Thanks, Mom. Thanks, Helen the rabbit."

The next day I looked for Helen in the garage. I wanted to hug the rabbit for helping me with my hole in one. She wasn't there. I put rabbit food out on the back steps every day, and every day she would come and eat the food when we couldn't see her. I was very sad, because I thought I would never see Helen again. Sometimes miracles take a little more time than you would like. I did see Helen again in my backyard. The miracle of miracles was that hundreds of other rabbits showed up. In a place where rabbits never lived, we now had a ton of them. Helen had brought her friends to be part of our life. I bet they were her friends from heaven. I am sure one of them was Dad. The coyotes stayed away. The rabbits survived.

Sometimes I hear the tall grass while it moves. I'm sure it's Helen letting me know she will always be with us. Even if she chose to return as a bunny rabbit!

XOXOXO

I believe in miracles, because the story I just told you is true. Every word of it! Moms and Dads leave us too early sometimes. God only gives us one each of these very, very special people. So tonight before you fall asleep, give them the biggest hug you can. Say, "Thank you and I love you." Someday they won't be here any longer. Just hope that their ghost will come to visit you.

THE END

PS Mom, I didn't forget what you told me. I wrote a book. Your story. I love you.

Lightning Source UK Ltd.
Milton Keynes UK
UKRC011402200119
335667UK00003B/1

9 781949 483420